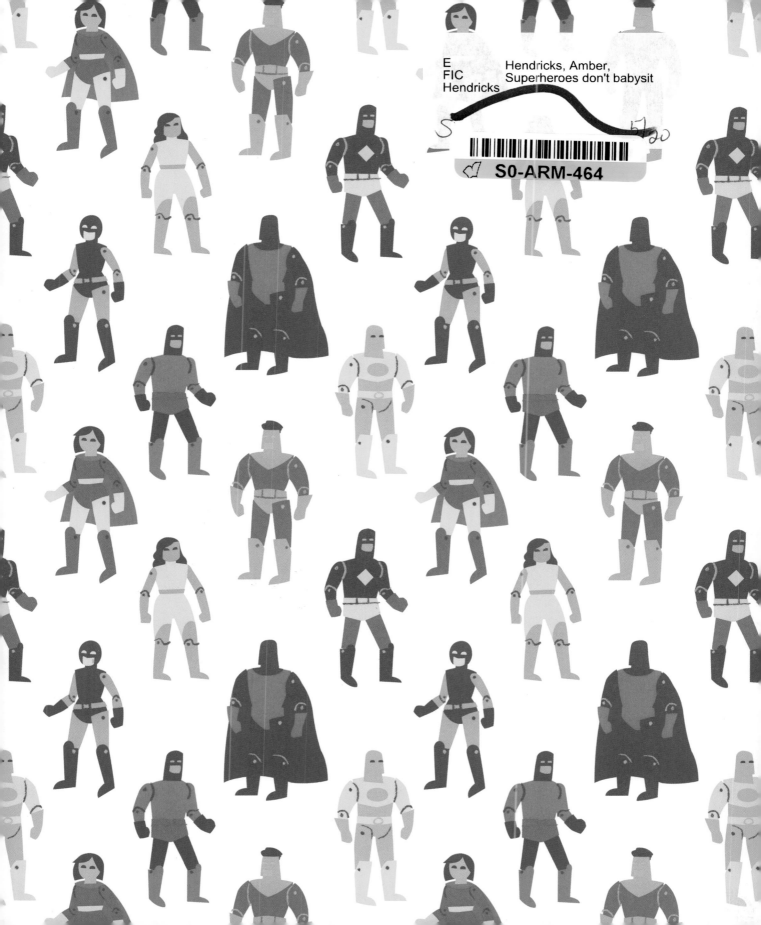

SUPERHEROES DON'T BABYSIT

by Amber Hendricks

illustrated by
Kyle Reed

beaming
books
beamingbooks.com

To Lochlan Reid, my very own superhero.
—A.H.

Text copyright © 2020 Amber Hendricks
Illustration copyright © 2020 Beaming Books

Published in 2020 by Beaming Books, an imprint of 1517 Media.
All rights reserved. No part of this book may be reproduced
without the written permission of the publisher.
Email copyright@1517.media. Printed in the United States of America.

26 25 24 23 22 21 20   1 2 3 4 5 6 7 8 9

ISBN: 978-1-5064-5876-2

Written by Amber Hendricks
Illustrated by Kyle Reed
Collage photo credits:
    Page 2: Tom Kelley Archive/iStock
    Page 7: gisele/iStock
    Page 26: atlantic-kid/iStock
    Page 27: gisele/iStock

Library of Congress Cataloging-in-Publication Data
Names: Hendricks, Amber, author. | Reed, Kyle, illustrator.
Title: Superheroes don't babysit / by Amber Hendricks ; illustrated by Kyle
    Reed.
Description: Minneapolis : Beaming Books, 2020. | Audience: Ages 5-8. |
    Summary: In the middle of saving the city, a superhero is asked to keep
    an eye on her little brother.
Identifiers: LCCN 2019034720 | ISBN 9781506458762 (hardcover)
Subjects: CYAC: Babysitters--Fiction. | Brothers and sisters--Fiction. |
    Superheroes--Fiction. | Humorous stories.
Classification: LCC PZ7.1.H4633 Sup 2020 | DDC [E]--dc23
LC record available at https://lccn.loc.gov/2019034720

VN0004589; 9781506458762; APR2020

Beaming Books
510 Marquette Avenue
Minneapolis, MN 55402
Beamingbooks.com

You'll be saving the city from the evil Emperor Zog when . . .

your dad asks for a favor.
A really big favor.
The **BIGGEST** of all **BIG** favors.

He'll ask you to . . .

. . . keep an eye on your little brother!

Of course, you won't want to.

You have plans, after all.

Plans that don't include

little brothers.

Besides,
SUPERHEROES DON'T BABYSIT.

You'll agree on the terms.

RIGHT AWAY,
your little brother will get hungry.

You'll check the list of Dad-approved snacks
(because superheroes follow the rules)
and fix him a plate of cheese and crackers.

But he'll want an ice cream sundae, and he'll insist on getting the ingredients himself.

He'll want to help measure and pour, squirt and scoop.

You'll feel **PROUD** . . .

until you notice
THE MESS.

Before you can clean up,
you'll smell something.
SOMETHING STINKY.

You'll check the normal places—the trash can, the bathroom,
your socks—before realizing the smell is coming from . . .

YOUR LITTLE BROTHER!

You'll put on the proper safety gear.

Changing your brother is tricky

WORSE THAN YOU IMAGINE.

But you figure it out.

Sort of.

Afterward, he'll ask to play with your dolls.

You'll explain that they are action figures, not dolls.
And they are **OFF LIMITS!**

BUT HE WON'T LISTEN!

There will be an **"INCIDENT."**

He'll start to cry.

You'll feel like crying, too.

You might even want to shout,

"I WISH YOU WEREN'T MY BROTHER!"

HE'LL HUG YOU

and say he's sorry.

He'll bring you his favorite teddy bear.
The one with the missing ear.

And that icky feeling inside
will melt away.

MAYBE little brothers
aren't so bad after all.

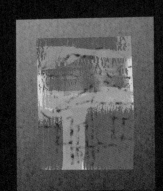

Soon he'll get sleepy.
He'll ask you to read him his favorite story.

SIX TIMES.

He'll fall asleep against you.
You'll know because he will drool on your arm.

But you won't mind.

MUCH.

BESIDES,
EVERY SUPERHERO NEEDS A SIDEKICK.

AMBER HENDRICKS is a children's book author based in Missouri. Amber has worn many hats in her career: army wife, mother, visual merchandiser, certified pharmacy technician, and most recently, childcare professional, but she has always circled back to her first love of telling stories. In addition to *Superheroes Don't Babysit*, Amber is the author of *Sophie and Little Star* and *Extraordinary Ordinary Ella*.

KYLE REED is an illustrator based in Hamilton, Ontario. His digital and traditional collage work has appeared in children's books, magazines, and advertising. In addition to *Superheroes Don't Babysit*, Kyle is the illustrator of *Three Little Birds* by Lysa Mullady. Kyle was also a part of CORE Digital Pictures' 2D design team working on *Super Why*, the children's educational cartoon.